U0538483

王亞茹 著
李魁賢 譯
Poems by Wang Ya-ru
Translated by Lee Kuei-shien

淡水河邊

Beside The Tamsui River

王亞茹漢英雙語詩集
Chinese - English

台灣詩叢 • Taiwan Poetry Series 26

【總序】詩推台灣印象

叢書策劃／李魁賢

　　進入21世紀，台灣詩人更積極走向國際，個人竭盡所能，在詩人朋友熱烈參與支持下，策畫出席過印度、蒙古、古巴、智利、緬甸、孟加拉、尼加拉瓜、馬其頓、秘魯、突尼西亞、越南、希臘、羅馬尼亞、墨西哥等國舉辦的國際詩歌節，並編輯《台灣心聲》等多種詩選在各國發行，使台灣詩人心聲透過作品傳佈國際間。

　　多年來進行國際詩交流活動最困擾的問題，莫如臨時編輯帶往國外交流的選集，大都應急處理，不但時間緊迫，且選用作品難免會有不周。因此，興起策畫【台灣詩叢】雙語詩系的念頭。若台灣詩人平常就有雙語詩集出版，隨時可以應用，詩作交流與詩人交誼雙管齊下，更具實際成效，對台灣詩的國際交流活動，當更加順利。

　　以【台灣】為名，著眼點當然有鑑於台灣文學在國際間名目不彰，台灣詩人能夠有機會在國際努力開拓空間，非為個人建立知名度，而是為推展台灣意象的整體事功，期待開創台灣文學的長久景象，才能奠定寶貴的歷史意義，台灣文學終必在世界文壇上佔有地位。

實際經驗也明顯印證，台灣詩人參與國際詩交流活動，很受重視，帶出去的詩選集也深受歡迎，從近年外國詩人和出版社與本人合作編譯台灣詩選，甚至主動翻譯本人詩集在各國文學雜誌或詩刊發表，進而出版外譯詩集的情況，大為增多，即可充分證明。

　　承蒙秀威資訊科技公司一本支援詩集出版初衷，慨然接受【台灣詩叢】列入編輯計畫，對台灣詩的國際交流，提供推進力量，希望能有更多各種不同外語的雙語詩集出版，形成進軍國際的集結基地。

目次

CONTENTS

3　【總序】詩推台灣印象／李魁賢

9　走過妳的詩・Walking by Your Poem
10　期望與失望・Expectations and Disappointments
11　妳叫淡水・Your are Called Tamsui
12　情繫淡水・My Beloved Tamsui
13　愛在忠寮・Love in Tiong-liâu
14　眺望淡水・Looking out Tamsui
15　我的情人花・My Lover Flower
16　淡水雨情・Rainy Affection in Tamsui
17　在你懷裡・In Your Arms
18　愛護淡水河・Take Care of the Tamsui River
19　冬季問候・Greetings in Winter Season
20　自我成長・Self Growth
21　曲中人・The Character in the Song
22　愛心・Love in Heart
23　寒露・Solar Term of Cold Dew
24　家味・Hometown Taste
25　頑強的草・Tenacious Grass
26　抗議・Protest
27　婚姻・The Marriage
28　親愛的・Darling

淡水河邊
Beside The Tamsui River

29　學會知足・Learn to be Content
30　遺言・Last Words
31　為和平吶喊・Shout for Peace
32　媽媽的心情・Mother's Mood
33　藥膏・Ointment
34　愛自己・Love Yourself
35　放下・Put Down
36　你是個寶・You Are a Treasure
37　病房裡聲音・Sounds in the Ward
38　幸福・Happiness
39　努力・Effort
40　沉思・Meditation
41　心靜・The Mind Calmed Down
42　傻女人・Fool Woman
43　隨妳・Follow You
44　詩的陶冶・The Edification of Poetry
45　漫步淡水河岸・Stroll Along the Tamsui Riverbank
46　紅樓印象・Impression on Red Castle
47　快樂詩歌節・Happy Poetry Festival
48　讀你・To Read You
49　遠的妳近的妳・You Afar, You Nearby
50　度日如年・Spending Day like Year

51	表述	Expression
52	生活	Life
53	夢	In Dream
54	你	You
55	真愛	Authentic Love
56	等待你	Waiting for You
57	忍耐	Endurance
58	孩子，我們明白	Kids, We Get It
59	居服工作者	To Home Care Workers
60	感言	My Feeling
61	你不笑我會哭	I Will Cry If You Don't Laugh
62	作者簡介	About the Poetess
63	譯者簡介	About the Translator

淡水河邊
Beside The Tamsui River

走過妳的詩

走過妳的詩
想起妳的名字——淡水
在世界的盡頭認識妳
妳的故事奇特動人
以世界眼睛看妳
妳風情萬種
使人愛上妳
妳的多元文化
外來人口都能適應
但妳明確告訴世人
不許破壞一磚一瓦
一樹一木一草一花
存在直到永遠

淡水河邊
Beside The Tamsui River

期望與失望

期望越高失望越多
只有我知道
多一份愛多一份急救
我不想身體增加拖磨
我不再期望未來
多一份奇蹟
只希望多一份安詳
請不要難過
或許順其自然
心裡就會坦然

妳叫淡水

以前人叫妳滬尾
現在人叫妳淡水
妳的名聲勝於響亮民謠
著名美麗島
外出人尋找妳
愛情故事中愛戀妳
為了印證
我要讀懂妳
航海史地圖上有妳
通往世界的大門
福爾摩莎名字
四百多年不曾變動
妳牽動台灣歷史
北台灣的經濟命脈
創下繁華年代
西式的教育、醫療在此扎根
如今的妳是歷史觀光港口
──金色水岸

淡水河邊
Beside The Tamsui River

情繫淡水

走過路留下我的足跡
在此生活繫結我的情感
我一生簡單行囊
來到淡水停泊
做個全新自我
我的夢在淡水開始
情感、工作、生活、家庭、孩子
在此實現我的成就
淡水呀！
妳是我永遠的故鄉

愛在忠寮

住在忠寮
生活在忠寮
我處處感覺
忠寮人的熱情
忠寮歷史悠久
一種人文氣質吸引
我定下永生情意
愛在忠寮

淡水河邊
Beside The Tamsui River

眺望淡水

美麗淡水歷史長流
河水注入台灣海峽
紅毛城歷經洗禮
西治時期　荷治時期　鄭氏時期
清治時期　日治時期　戰後時期
文化古蹟見證歷史變遷
眺望海天之間
耳邊盈滿觀音的祝福
大屯山望著淡水河的輪渡
河面的夕陽在撒嬌
歌詠長調情感永恆
我眺望淡水河　默默
讚嘆　生命的此岸彼岸
恍若有橋相連

我的情人花

妳星星點綴庭院
裝飾我的眼睛
香氣淡雅宜人
那種感覺如我的情人
給予我香氣享受
我吸足它的美感
它的歷史它的生命
價值千金
內心的活力
一次次激觸我
我醉了
醉於妳的美感芳香
讓我為妳舞動為妳喜悅

淡水河邊
Beside The Tamsui River

淡水雨情

雨一直下
淡水情如雨絲
遊客們
遊淡水的情思不曾減弱
媽媽載孩子去學校
阿伯阿桑趕市集
年輕人也總是
認真打拚
淡水的雨情
展現淡水人的精神
更是淡水的一道風景

在你懷裡

溫暖擁抱你
在歸途的河岸
油膩作伴
讓我捨去一身疲勞
偎在你懷裡
謝謝你
鬱金香酒店

淡水河邊
Beside The Tamsui River

愛護淡水河

私人遊艇，渡輪
淡水河上慶祝party
行駛
親愛的遊客們
謝謝你們來遊玩
請不要亂丟垃圾亂吐口水
我是完美無瑕的河流
要做好防洪防污
城市的美與發展少不了我
我不想嘗試海綿城市的殘
我們城市有著河川與水
共存美
記住來淡水河遊玩
多對我微笑
多拍幾張相片留念
我會記住你來過淡水河

冬季問候

朋友好
在這一年末
謹致上真誠問候
我們送走春夏秋季
迎來寒冬
冬季是我們總結季節
或許我們所失所得
不如意
但我們坦誠面對
成長壯大
給予我們大大擁抱
愛自己

自我成長

成長是過程
但我們有把握嗎？
說不定
父母生孩子養大是責任
孩子長大是自己責任
勿養成父母照顧孩子永遠
沒完沒了
成長道路要靠自己
靠山吃山空
靠父母，父母會倒
靠自己比較實在
經歷與過程有待磨練
自己的人生道路不跨出
永遠不知道外面的世界
豔陽高照

曲中人

強表現灑脫
經歷往事
滿身傷痕累累
但勇敢走出圍牆
心胸坦蕩蕩
以稻草之韌性
努力、奮鬥、堅強
鋪築一片綠地
人生道路總有些包袱
放下吧
對著曲中的我說
妳最棒！妳要加油！

愛心

愛在心
一直都在
我對你的愛
在心中縈繞不斷
愛你
你是否依然愛我
你的笑容　你的溫度　你的懷抱
永遠在心頭
忘不了

寒露

深秋氣息越來越濃
清晨寒
已在枝葉結冰
山頭的楓葉漸變紅
一滴寒露點點紅
已是深秋
現在的你還好嗎？

淡水河邊
Beside The Tamsui River

家味

母親在世時
回家路近
母親不在了
回家路途遙遠
夢裡
母親準備一大桌
家鄉味
「快吃，這都是你們愛吃的味！」

頑強的草

你
總是一次次遇見困難挫折
但
相信一切都會過去
不擔心未來
對於發生的事
無論好與壞
開心與憂慮
都會
張開雙手熱忱擁抱
堅定信心會遇見更好的未來
努力面對生活

淡水河邊
Beside The Tamsui River

抗議

無聲
你穿越人體
擊敗人類
在世界各國裡
蔓延
無數的悲痛聲
抗議
你善變
但我相信
人類會戰勝你

婚姻

婚姻盡頭
傷痕累累
淚流成河
各自飛
換取一份自由
解脫
謝謝婚姻洗禮

淡水河邊
Beside The Tamsui River

親愛的

親愛的
秋冬即將到來
希望我的問候
溫暖你的心情
希望今天的你每天的你
心情美麗　一切順心
簡單的問候
是心靈深處的感覺
美好的事事
也許不會處處與我們相伴
但我們用心真心
對待過洗禮過
總會有光的感觸
一切一切在不言中

學會知足

比較少些　知足多些
要擁有
不被外界打擾的能力
少關注他人
把注意力集在
讓自己感到快樂

淡水河邊
Beside The Tamsui River

遺言

沒有希望就失去勇氣
給再多的營養蛋白質
只是維持氣息
但我久病臥床
生命無意義
只想早點解脫
寬容的人間愛
我無福享受
感謝了

為和平吶喊

人民享受和平　溫暖
不喜歡戰火　硝煙
討厭霸道獨裁
什麼共產主義
騙人
請還人民
一個自由民主

淡水河邊
Beside The Tamsui River

媽媽的心情

媽媽很偉大
永遠是孩子後盾
八十幾歲母親
急診區守候六十幾歲兒子
夜裡
看著滿頭白髮母親
眼珠佈滿血絲
但眼神有力直看著
急診區恢復室的門
心裡為兒子加油打氣
「加油！我的寶貝兒子！」
我同樣身為母親
心裡感受萬分
我的孩子感冒咳嗽時
我的心情也是如此

藥膏

老太太洗完澡
「王小姐」
「幫我拿貼布藥膏」
「好！簡媽，妳這貼布有效嗎？」
「沒辦法，女兒孝心買的！」
「對喔！貼心安的哈哈哈哈哈！」
啊！活到這把年紀子女孝順就好
不希望需求什麼
也不會變年輕
事事平安就好
子女孝順
求得好死不受病痛折磨最好

淡水河邊
Beside The Tamsui River

愛自己

生活不幸
疾病折磨
我知道你很累
你想放棄一切
跟隨天使
但
你想過孩子　家人嗎
家人的關心與愛
孩子依你榜樣
你拿什麼回報
你現在唯一能做的
聽醫生的話
好好治療
未來日子裡
好好陪家人孩子

放下

談容易
但真要放下難
我夜晚用淚澆醒自己
該做的治療已經做過
我的孩子還小
不能放棄
我盡我所能努力
跟病魔拚一拚
希望能夠戰勝病魔

淡水河邊
Beside The Tamsui River

你是個寶

遠視近觀
你總是平易近人
風趣幽默
話語頻率讓我心醉
心中的琴弦只為你彈
我會晨昏日夜想你
把你當成我心靈的歸岸
讓我成長

病房裡聲音

我要喝糖水
重覆講數不清幾次
啊……
我要坐飛機出國
阿爸、阿母、阿弟、阿妹
我錢在衣櫥裡
我的金子幫我戴上
這樣的話
在病房裡聽N次
沒人覺得奇怪
習慣了
失智病友阿嬤的話
可以講天南地北
講金銀珠寶
死裡哀求話也有
出口成章
病房裡的聲音一種節拍
讚美阿嬤
丹田有力

淡水河邊
Beside The Tamsui River

幸福

老的,妳講什麼
我聽不到
你的紅包全部給我
不行
女兒給我的
我要留這做老本
你啊什麼老本
還不是花我的……

努力

自己努力才可幫助自己
別人的幫助有限
生活上的不幸
不是我們想要的
但我們坦然接受
想想妳還年輕
才六十幾
不要什麼都靠老公
中風不可怕
可怕的是妳不積極做復健
我照顧過
像妳這樣例子很多
中風初期努力做復健
很可能康復
湯小姐
妳要加油努力
希望
下次看到妳時大有進步

淡水河邊
Beside The Tamsui River

沉思

握著手中相片
奶奶沉思片刻
奶奶妳還好嗎？
我很好
謝謝妳王小姐
奶奶眼中淚水泛花
我靜默
也許失去人生的至親最愛
剩下的就是沉思
今生緣份已盡
隔著風隔著雨
天涯路
從此無相逢
留在
心底的夢
心底的風
種在記憶裡

心靜

聆賞一曲音樂
讓心田放鬆
灌滿無數美好旋律
閱讀一首詩
讓自己心靜
帶動人生季節旋律
讓我無盡喜悅
靜心譜寫
詩　情　畫　意

淡水河邊
Beside The Tamsui River

傻女人

追夢而來
想找夢中感覺
但錯啦
處處是傷口
檢討
千百次錯誤
千百次希望
但錯誤永遠是錯誤
希望總是變成失望
承載無數淚水
傻女人醒了
珍重離別
珍惜自己
愛恨不再重演

隨妳

在天邊
我化成風跟隨妳
我越過大海
伴妳春　夏　秋　冬
看日出日落
我關心妳
眼裡的風景
全是妳

淡水河邊
Beside The Tamsui River

詩的陶冶

身穿適應季節的衣裳
著手寫出詩意
世間的人情
繁華　美麗　沒落
唯獨詩釋然自我
偶爾伴樂舞步
自我陶冶
對於世界的五顏六色
勇敢表態
哪怕是站在舞台邊角
也感覺有價值
存在

漫步淡水河岸

黃昏雨絲相伴
河岸遊客滿滿
閒聊淡水故事
過去　現在　未來
憧憬一切的美好
淚水　笑語
仰望觀音山
祈求
保平安

淡水河邊
Beside The Tamsui River

紅樓印象

階梯
層層堅固卵石
步步高升
古建築
留下
多一份記憶
多一份情感
人事景物　印象
不時回味
先人留下的美
詩人思古幽情

快樂詩歌節

不同情感連結在一起
祝福你　祝福我　祝福我們
不同的語言
不同的國度
不同的膚色
舞動快樂腳步
芬芳感染

淡水河邊
Beside The Tamsui River

讀你

我要讀你千百遍
天上的明月如你
在黑暗裡給我光
你如春天的陽光
愛的絢麗花芯
我從春天走到冬天
為找尋你等待你
你是美麗的傳說
一種迷魂的芳味
值得我愛戴

遠的妳近的妳

最遠的妳是最近的妳
遙知而近；近知而親
劇場裡的主角
光與愛被釋懷
遠射的燈光暫停頓
目睹伊人的妳
永遠幸運伴隨妳
妳用五彩的繽紛譜曲生活
妳用五穀的雜糧陪伴生活
妳用甘甜的乳汁醞釀生活
妳用味覺和視覺品嚐生活
妳的人生五彩勝於黑白
前人後人不會忘記妳
妳會在地球留下腳印

淡水河邊
Beside The Tamsui River

度日如年

秒針滴答滴答輪轉
季節的風聲讓你感到無味
窗外陽光時而明媚時而哭泣
在這度日如年的日子裡
妳忘記自我忘記家人
但忘記不了自己的美夢
因為妳不管黃昏黑夜白天
都昏昏大睡
生命的呼吸器無止盡消耗
趨向盡頭的終點
也是心靈的寄託

表述

不言不語
不代表沉默
心在表述
肢體語言在講話
眾人的眼神會見證
自我意識的認可與否認
請勿用虛偽的妝扮畫押
我心堅定
不管你在背後吆喝
自我陶醉
可笑

淡水河邊
Beside The Tamsui River

生活

生活一捉襟就見肘
生活纏綿於柴米油鹽
雪霜滿頭罩
衣衫照舊沒有新花樣
銀兩不夠
生活依然無奈
丟了青春輸了歲月
留下愛

夢

夢
想念你
把無數呼吸卡住我喉結
你的吻你的擁抱
你的愛掐住我
是那麼的火熱
讓我火山爆發

淡水河邊
Beside The Tamsui River

你

一段記憶又一段記憶
給我畫圓圈刻板加深
生怕記憶少了你
無論是風的季節
影像搖晃
你總是第一個問候我的人
我早已銘刻我心
我想長久擁有你
但我明白流星是瞬間的美
只能種植在記憶裡
我寧可用前世的愛
換取今生的相逢

真愛

愛不在乎長久或短暫
愛不是承諾山高水長
而是久別重逢後
一重回憶刻骨銘心的愛
真實的精神支柱
永遠的精神糧食
或許平淡
但的確給予你成長哲理
真愛在我身邊

淡水河邊
Beside The Tamsui River

等待你

青春的等待又剛烈又柔和
但有一種等待是想你
你不是天上的星星和月亮
也不是人間的神明
但你有一種神奇的力量吸引
不時為你思念
不分白天和夜晚
等待著你的雙肩
在地球的一個角落
等待你

忍耐

一場婚姻
磨消女人的氣
數著星星月亮過日子
把溫柔氣質的女孩
變成潑婦
往事只能回味
但女人身上往事
不敢回味
躲在微薄空間裡舔傷口
哭過傷過女人覺醒
還有孩子存在
還有自己生命存在
哭一哭笑一笑就好
快樂幸福曙光在前方

淡水河邊
Beside The Tamsui River

孩子，我們明白

孩子你們長大
我們老了
你們每次都很忙
工作　生活　家庭
但我們做父母活在你空間
佔住一角
我們老了不要講太多語言
不要管太多閒事
你們講的話我們未必懂
我們講的話你們未必聽
但我們有顆愛你們的心
父母對孩子的愛如牛毛那麼多
孩子對父母的愛如剪牛毛那麼短

居服工作者

妳們每天
穿越社區　鄉間
做居服工作
走進長者家裡關心長照
迎風雨妳們微笑
對陽光妳們高歌
聽長者的心與情
訴說昨天與今天故事
長者飯菜裡飄香居服味道
醫院檢診有居服陪伴
復健功課裡
妳們一把手一把腳
鼓勵長者動起來
身體清潔長者喜愛
臥床長者須翻身拍背
那扣背聲宛如華爾滋歌曲
在鼓舞

淡水河邊
Beside The Tamsui River

感言

照顧過看過無數的長者
陪著聽著他們講昨天今天過去故事
最後我心痛糾結
他們從走動到使用助行器
從輪椅到臥床
人的老化說不定
也許經過會急速老化
但居家照顧的這條路滿長
有時候我們要理解
今天我願意照顧別人
我們有一天需要時
也希望別人可以好好對待我們

你不笑我會哭

每週星期三下午
是朱媽媽安全陪伴時間
「朱媽媽這幾天有卡好沒」
老人家
用慈祥笑臉看著我
我不想看到她長期臥床
想要她動起來
不想讓她整天靠流質維持生命
想要她生命活得有意義
「朱媽
妳吞嚥功能要訓練
手腳的肌力張力要訓練
居家復健師有來吧」
「有」
「那就好　這樣我卡放心
心情要放輕鬆多笑笑
我對妳滿滿的希望
妳不笑我會哭」

作者簡介

　　王亞茹，1981 年出生於海南島，在台灣長期從事長照服務已超過十年。善於舞蹈，曾獲 2019 年新住民舞蹈比賽佳作獎。2018 年開始寫詩，在《笠》詩刊發表。出版詩集《居服員對白》（2021 年）和《我在淡水》（2023 年）。

譯者簡介

　　李魁賢（1937-2025），已出版 62 本不同語文的詩集，包括華文、日文、英文、葡萄牙文、蒙古文、羅馬尼亞文、俄文、西班牙文、法文、韓文、孟加拉文、塞爾維亞文、土耳其文、阿爾巴尼亞文、阿拉伯文、德文和印地文。詩創作成就獲得吳濁流新詩獎、巫永福文學評論獎、榮後台灣詩獎、賴和文學獎、行政院文化獎、吳三連獎新詩獎、真理大學台灣文學家牛津獎、國家文藝獎，和許多國際獎項，包含印度、蒙古、韓國、孟加拉、馬其頓、秘魯、蒙特內哥羅、塞爾維亞和美國等國。

淡水河邊
Beside The Tamsui River

英語篇

CONTENTS

71	Walking by Your Poem・走過妳的詩	
72	Expectations and Disappointments・期望與失望	
73	Your are Called Tamsui・妳叫淡水	
74	My Beloved Tamsui・情繫淡水	
75	Love in Tiong-liâu・愛在忠寮	
76	Looking out Tamsui・眺望淡水	
77	My Lover Flower・我的情人花	
78	Rainy Affection in Tamsui・淡水雨情	
79	In Your Arms・在你懷裡	
80	Take Care of the Tamsui River・愛護淡水河	
81	Greetings in Winter Season・冬季問候	
82	Self Growth・自我成長	
83	The Character in the Song・曲中人	
84	Love in Heart・愛心	
85	Solar Term of Cold Dew・寒露	
86	Hometown Taste・家味	
87	Tenacious Grass・頑強的草	
88	Protest・抗議	
89	The Marriage・婚姻	
90	Darling・親愛的	
91	Learn to be Content・學會知足	
92	Last Words・遺言	

淡水河邊
Beside The Tamsui River

93	Shout for Peace・為和平吶喊
94	Mother's Mood・媽媽的心情
95	Ointment・藥膏
96	Love Yourself・愛自己
97	Put Down・放下
98	You Are a Treasure・你是個寶
99	Sounds in the Ward・病房裡聲音
100	Happiness・幸福
101	Effort・努力
102	Meditation・沉思
103	The Mind Calmed Down・心靜
104	Fool Woman・傻女人
105	Follow You・隨妳
106	The Edification of Poetry・詩的陶冶
107	Stroll Along the Tamsui Riverbank・漫步淡水河岸
108	Impression on Red Castle・紅樓印象
109	Happy Poetry Festival・快樂詩歌節
110	To Read You・讀妳
111	You Afar, You Nearby・遠的妳近的妳
112	Spending Day like Year・度日如年
113	Expression・表述
114	Life・生活

CONTENTS

115　In Dream・夢
116　You・你
117　Authentic Love・真愛
118　Waiting for You・等待你
119　Endurance・忍耐
120　Kids, We Get It・孩子，我們明白
121　To Home Care Workers・居服工作者
122　My Feeling・感言
123　I Will Cry If You Don't Laugh・你不笑我會哭

124　About the Poetess・作者簡介
125　About the Translator・譯者簡介

淡水河邊
Beside The Tamsui River

Walking by Your Poem

Walking by your poem

I am reminded of your name - Tamsui.

I know you at the end of the world,

your story is peculiar and touching.

Seeing you with the eyes of the world

you show various fascination that

makes people falling in love with you.

Your multicultural

makes the population from outside able to adapt.

But you tell the people in the world clearly

not allowed to destroy one brick, one tile,

one tree, one wood, one grass, one flower,

let them exist until forever.

淡水河邊
Beside The Tamsui River

Expectations and Disappointments

The higher expectations, the more disappointments,
only I know that
one more love given, one more first aid needed.
I don't want to increase suffering on my body.
I have no longer expectation for
one more miracle in the future
just hope one more serenity.
Please don't be sad,
maybe let nature take its course,
then my heart will be calm.

Your are Called Tamsui

You are earlier called Hobe,
now you are called Tamsui.
Your fame is superior over a prestigious ballad,
the famous "Beautiful Island".
The people going outside are looking for you
and love you in the love story.
In order to make witness
I want to understand you through reading.
On the map of maritime history,
your name of Formosa
is the gate toward the world
unchanged for more than four hundred years.
You impacted Taiwanese history
on economic lifeline of northern Taiwan
to create a prosperous era.
Western education and medical care took root here,
nowadays you are a historical tourist port
— Golden Coast.

淡水河邊
Beside The Tamsui River

My Beloved Tamsui

I walked on the road and left my footprints,
I lived here in combination with my emotions.
My all life just with a simple luggage
arrived at Tamsui to moor here
as a complete new ego.
My dream began in Tamsui,
emotions, work, life, family, child,
and have realized my achievements here.
Oh, Tamsui!
You are my eternal hometown.

Love in Tiong-liâu

I live in Tiong-liâu.
I spend my living in Tiong-liâu.
I feel everywhere
the enthusiasm of Tiong-liâu people.
Tiong-liâu has a long history,
a kind of humanistic temperament attracts me.
I settle here with eternal affection,
love in Tiong-liâu.

淡水河邊
Beside The Tamsui River

Looking out Tamsui

Beautiful Tamsui has a long stream of history
with river water flowing into the Taiwan Strait.
The Fort San Domingo has been baptized through
Spanish ruling period, Dutch ruling period, Koxinga period,
Qing ruling period, Japanese ruling period, post-war period.
Cultural monuments have witnessed the historical changes.
During looking out between the sea and sky
my ears are filled with blessings from Guanyin Goddess.
Mount Datun looks out the ferry boats crossing Tamsui River,
the sunset on the surface of river is acting coquette,
sings long tune displaying eternal emotions.
I look out Tamsui River in silence,
amazed by this shore and other shore of life
as if connected by a bridge.

My Lover Flower

You the stars embellish the garden,
decorate my eyes,
with an aroma light elegant and pleasant.
That sense like my lover
providing me the enjoyment of fragrance.
I suck sufficient your aesthetic feeling,
your history and your life
worth a thousand pieces of gold.
Your inner vitality
inspires me again and again.
I am drunk
intoxicated by your aesthetic feeling and fragrance.
Let me dance for you and make you happy.

淡水河邊
Beside The Tamsui River

Rainy Affection in Tamsui

It keeps raining,
affections in Tamsui are like drizzles.
The travelers have never reduced
their affections for traveling to Tamsui.
The mothers take their children to school,
old uncles and old aunts go to the market,
young people are always
work hard seriously.
Rainy Affection in Tamsui
displays the spirit of people living in Tamsui,
even more a scenery in Tamsui.

In Your Arms

Warmth hugs you
beside river bank on the way home,
there is grease as a companion
let me get rid of fatigue on all my body.
I nestle in your arms,
oh, Golden Tulip Hotel,
thank you!

淡水河邊
Beside The Tamsui River

Take Care of the Tamsui River

Private yachts and ferries
navigate on the Tamsui River to hold
celebration party.
Dear travelers
thank you for coming to visit,
but please don't litter and spit.
I am a flawless perfect river
without me cannot do well prevent floods and pollution
to keep beauty and development of the city.
I would not to try the remnants of Sponge City,
our city has rivers and water
together to keep the beauty existed.
Remember coming to visit the Tamsui River,
smiling more at me,
taking some more photos as souvenirs.
I will remember you having come to the Tamsui River.

Greetings in Winter Season

Hello, my friends,

at the end of this year

I send my sincere regards!

We say farewell to spring, summer and autumn,

welcoming cold winter.

The winter is our summary season,

maybe our loss and our gain

are unsatisfactory

but we face it honestly

in order to grow and stronger

and give us a big hug

love ourself.

淡水河邊
Beside The Tamsui River

Self Growth

Growth is a process

But are we sure?

Maybe

the parents have responsibility to give birth and raise children,

the children have their own responsibility to grow up,

not rely the parents to take care of them forever

without an end.

The growth path depends on oneself,

the backer eats up the mountain to emptiness.

Rely on parents, the parents will fall,

it's more practical to rely on oneself.

Experience and process need to be tempered,

if not step out on your own life path

you will never know in the outside world

the sun shines brightly.

The Character in the Song

To barely perform free and easy
past experiences
make all body full of scars.
But when step out of the wall bravely
with open-mind
by toughness of straw
working hard, struggle, strong
will pave to finish a large green land.
There is always some baggages in the road of life
put it down!
Told me, being the character in the song:
You are the best! You must keep to work hard!

淡水河邊
Beside The Tamsui River

Love in Heart

Love in heart
always has been there.
My love to you
lingers in my heart continuously.
I love you,
do you still love me?
Your smile, your warmth, your hug
always remain in my heart
unforgettable.

Solar Term of Cold Dew

The atmosphere of late autumn is getting stronger.
Cold in the early morning
has frozen on the branches and leaves.
The maple leaves on the hilltops gradually turn red.
A drop of cold dew presents a lot of red dots.
It is already late autumn,
are you all right now?

淡水河邊
Beside The Tamsui River

Hometown Taste

When mother was alive

the way home is very close-by.

Now, mother has gone

the way home becomes far away.

In my dream

mother prepares a prosperous table of

hometown taste

"Go ahead to eat, these are all your favorite flavor!"

Tenacious Grass

You
always encounter difficulties and setbacks again and again
but
believe everything will pass away,
not worry about the future.
To what happened
wether good or bad
joy or worry
you will
open your hands to give enthusiastic hug.
The firm confidence will lead to a better future
endeavoring to face living.

淡水河邊
Beside The Tamsui River

Protest

Silently
you pass through the human body,
defeat human being,
extending
in various countries of the world.
Countless sounds of sorrow
protest
your fickleness
but I believe
human being will win over you.

The Marriage

The marriage at the end
is full of scars
with tears streaming like a river.
Go to separate way
in exchange for freedom
to liberate.
Thanks to the baptism by marriage.

淡水河邊
Beside The Tamsui River

Darling

Darling

autumn and winter are coming,

I hope my regards

will warm your mood,

and hope you today and every day

beautiful mood going everything as you wish.

My simple greeting

is a feeling deep in the soul.

All good things

maybe not in accompany with us everywhere,

but we are wholeheartedly

to deal with and baptized.

There will always be a feeling of lighting,

all is in without a word.

Learn to be Content

Be lesser compared, more contented,
to possess the ability
without disturbed by outside world
and pay less attention to others,
had better concentrate on
making yourself feel happy.

淡水河邊
Beside The Tamsui River

Last Words

No hope will lose courage,
given more of nutritious protein
can only maintain breathing.
I have been bedridden for long disease,
my life is meaningless,
I just want to liberate as soon as possible.
I am not blessed to enjoy
tolerant love of human being.
Thanks a lot!

Shout for Peace

People enjoy peace and warmth,
dislike flames of war, gun smokes
disgust overbearing dictatorship.
What communism?
Liar!
Please revert the people
a liberal democracy.

淡水河邊
Beside The Tamsui River

Mother's Mood

Mother is great,
always the back supporter of her children.
A mother over eighty years old
guards her son over sixties in the emergency area.
At night
I watch this mother with white hairs over all her head
and her eyeballs spread over bloodshot.
But her eyesight is energetic to stare at
the gate of recovery room at emergency area
and heartily encourages her son
"Keep it up! My baby son!"
I am the same a mother
feeling so much in my heart,
when my child gets a cold, has cough
my mood is also such the same.

Ointment

The old lady finished her bath,
"Miss Wang"
"Help me get the patch and ointment."
"Okay! Aunt Jane, is this patch effective?"
"I can't help, my daughter bought it by her filial mind!"
"Right! Use patch to get peace of mind, hahaha!"
Ah! Until this old age, it's good to have filial children,
I neither hope to ask for anything
nor possible to become younger,
but wish everything safe
and children all filial,
best to seek a good death without tortured by illness.

淡水河邊
Beside The Tamsui River

Love Yourself

Your living is unfortunately
tortured by sickness.
I know you are very tired,
you want to give up everything
following up the angel
but
have you thought about your children and family?
Family care and love,
children follow your example,
what do you give in return?
The only thing you can do now
is obedient to the doctor
getting well treatment,
in the future days
spending time with your family and children.

Put Down

It is easier to say
but difficult to put down in the real.
I wake myself up with pouring tears at night.
The necessary treatment has been done.
My child is still young,
can not be given up.
I try all my best
to fight against the disease
hoping to beat it.

淡水河邊
Beside The Tamsui River

You Are a Treasure

Whether look far or closer view
you are always approachable,
funny and humorous,
your frequency of wording makes me intoxicated.
The strings in my heart are played only for you,
I will miss you morning and evening, day and night
and treat you as the return shore of my soul
let me grow.

Sounds in the Ward

I want to drink sugar water,
I repeat to say it countless times.
Ah……
I want take airplane going abroad.
Oh, daddy, mommy, young brother, young sister,
my money is in the closet,
please help me to put on gold ornaments.
Such words
have been heard N times in the ward,
no one feels wonder
and gets used to.
The words from wardmate grandma of a dementia
can involve everything from the south to north,
about gold, silver and jewelry,
even the begging words from the dead
expressed fluently.
Sounds in the ward is regarded as a tempo
praising grandma
a powerful dān tián.

淡水河邊
Beside The Tamsui River

Happiness

Old partner, what are you saying?

I can not hear you.

Give me all your money received from red envelope!

No way!

It was daughter giving to me,

I want to save it as my old age money,

Oh you, what old age money?

Don't you spending my….

Effort

Only you by making own effort can help yourself
others helps are limited.
The misfortune happened in living
are not what we want
but we may accept it calmly.
I think about you being still young
only more than sixty years old
so don't rely on your husband for everything.
Suffering from stroke is not terrible,
What's scared is that you don't do active rehabilitation.
I have taken care of
many examples like you
making effort on rehabilitation in the initial stage of stroke
possibly to recover to good health.
Miss Tang
you have to do your best effort,
hope
great progress next time I see you.

淡水河邊
Beside The Tamsui River

Meditation

Holding photo tight in the hand
grandma meditates for a moment.
Grandma, are you okay?
I am fine,
thank you, Miss Wang!
Grandma filled with tears blurred in her eyes,
I keep silent.
Maybe got lost the most loved one in life,
only the meditation is remained.
The fate in this life is over,
separated by the wind and the rain,
the way to the end of world
will never encountered again.
The dreams that left in the bottom of heart,
the winds that left in the bottom of heart,
are all
planted in memory.

The Mind Calmed Down

To listen a song of music
let heart field relax
to irrigate full with countless beautiful melodies.
To read a poem
calm down yourself
to drive the seasonal melody of life.
Let me endless happy
to compose quietly
the poetic feeling and picturesque meaning.

淡水河邊
Beside The Tamsui River

Fool Woman

Come to chase dreams,
want to find the feeling in dreams.
But being wrong,
there are wounds everywhere.
By reviewing
thousand times of mistakes
and thousand times of hopes,
but the mistake is always mistake,
the hope always turns into disappointment.
Carrying countless tears
the fool woman wakes up
to say goodbye.
To cherish herself
never to love and hate again.

Follow You

On the margin of the sky
I turn into the wind to follow you.
I cross over the sea to accompany you
in spring, summer, autumn and winter,
watching the sunrise and sunset.
I take care about you,
the scenery in my eyes
all are you.

淡水河邊
Beside The Tamsui River

The Edification of Poetry

I wear clothes that suit the season
starting to write out poetical meaning.
The human touch in the world
prosperity, beauty, and decline
only poetry can take easy by itself,
occasionally dance to follow music
making self edification,
to express an opinion bravely
on colors of the world.
Even standing at the corner of the stage
I also feel valuable
to exist.

Stroll Along the Tamsui Riverbank

Accompanied by drizzle at dusk
the riverbank is full of tourists
chatting about Tamsui stories
past over, present, and in future.
Looking forward to having all beautiful
carrying tears and laughter
looking up at Mount Guanyin
praying
to keep peaceful safe.

淡水河邊
Beside The Tamsui River

Impression on Red Castle

The ladder

with rigid pebbles layer by layer,

goes up step by step.

The ancient building

has left behind with

one more memory

one more emotion.

The impressions on people, things, scenery

are recollected from time to time

about the beauty left behind by our ancestors

to remind poets the nostalgia for ancient times.

Happy Poetry Festival

Different emotions are connected together
blessing you, blessing me, blessing us.
Different languages
different countries
different skin colors
dance happy steps
getting aromatic infection.

淡水河邊
Beside The Tamsui River

To Read You

I want to read you a thousand times.
The bright moon in the sky is like you
giving me light in the darkness.
You are like the sunshine of spring time,
the gorgeous flower core of love.
I walked from spring to winter
for searching you, and waiting you.
You are a beautiful legend,
a kind of charming aroma
worthy of my love and esteem.

You Afar, You Nearby

What you most afar is you most nearby.

Know from afar but nearby, know at nearby but intimate.

As the protagonist in theater

light and love are relieved,

the distant projecting light is paused.

I witness you, my beloved lady,

fortune always accompanies you.

You compose your life with colorful tunes,

you accompany your life with whole grains,

you brew your life with sweet milk,

you try your life with taste and vision senses.

Your all life colorful is superior than black and white.

People before and after you will never forget you.

You will leave footprints on the earth.

淡水河邊
Beside The Tamsui River

Spending Day like Year

Second hand ticks, ticks and rotates.
The wind sound of season makes you feel tasteless.
The sunshine outside the window are sometimes bright or weeping.
In spending day like year
you forget yourself and your family
but can't forget your own fond dream,
because no matter dusk, night or day
you always fall into sound sleep.
The respirator of life is endlessly consumed,
as life approaches towards the terminus,
this is also the sustenance of the soul.

Expression

Without any word
does not represent silence,
the heart is in expression,
body language is speaking,
everyone's eyes will make witness.
Don't use hypocritical makeup to sign
recognition and denial of self-consciousness.
My heart is firm,
doesn't care about you shouting behind my back,
or self-intoxication,
laughable!

淡水河邊
Beside The Tamsui River

Life

Life is pulling collar to cause elbow bared.
Life is entangled with firewood, rice, oil and salt,
results snow frost covering over all head.
As usual there are no new patterns of clothes,
no enough money,
life is still helpless.
Lose youth, lose years
leave behind love.

In Dream

In dream

I miss you,

with countless breaths stuck in my Adam's apple.

enjoying your kiss, your hug.

Your love chokes me,

such fiery hot

making my volcano erupt.

淡水河邊
Beside The Tamsui River

You

One memory after another
draw me circles to engrave and deepen
that afraid of without you in my memory.
No matter during the wind season
shadows are wobbling,
you are always the first one to greet me.
I have already earlier impressed in my heart.
I want to have you for a long time
but I understand that shooting star is momentary beauty
can only be planted in memory.
I would rather use the love from my previous life
in exchange for encounter in this life.

Authentic Love

Love doesn't care long or short

Love doesn't promise to have high mountains and long rivers.

Rather when meeting again after a long separation

a layer of love memory has been engraved in the heart.

Real spiritual pillar

is eternal spiritual food

maybe bland

but does give you a philosophy of growth.

Authentic love is by my side.

淡水河邊
Beside The Tamsui River

Waiting for You

The waiting of youth is both strong and gentle
but there is a kind of waiting for missing you.
You are neither the stars and moon in the sky
nor a god in the human world,
but you have a magical power to attract.
I think you from time to time
regardless of day or night
waiting for your shoulders
in a corner of the earth,
waiting for you.

Endurance

One marriage

wears away the woman's angry

to live life in counting the stars and the moon.

The girl with gentle temperament

becomes a shrew.

The past events can only be recalled

but the past events on women body

are dared not to recall

hiding in a small space to lick wounds.

The woman awakes after crying and getting hurt,

there are still children existed,

there is still her own life existed,

just cry and laugh once is enough,

the morning light of joy and happiness lies ahead.

淡水河邊
Beside The Tamsui River

Kids, We Get It

Kids, you grow up,
we are old.
You are each time very busy for
work, life, family,
but as parents we live in your space
occupying a corner.
We old one shouldn't speak too much words,
don't be nosy too much.
We may not understand what you are saying,
you may not listen to what we say,
but we have a heart that loves you.
Parents love their children so much as cow hair,
kids love their parents as short as clipping cow hairs.

To Home Care Workers

Every day
you go through the communities and villages
to do home care works
entering the homes of elders for long-term attendance.
You smile to welcome the wind and rain,
sing loudly towards the sunshine,
and listen to the moods and feelings of the elders
talking about their stories of yesterday and today.
The foods for elders smell fragrance of home care,
hospital examination is accompanied by home care worker.
In teaching rehabilitation exercise
you move your hands and feet
encouraging the elders to take action.
You clean the elders' bodies to make them happy,
turn over the bedridden elders and pat their backs
that sounded like a Waltz music
to inspire them.

淡水河邊
Beside The Tamsui River

My Feeling

I have taken care and seen countless elders,
listened to their stories of yesterday and today,
at last my heart was in pain.
They move from walking to using the walker,
from by means of wheelchair to lie on bed.
The aging of human is not sured,
may be aged rapidly in the process,
but home care is a long way to take.
Sometimes we have to understand
I am willing to take care of others today
and hope others may treat us well
when we need someday.

I Will Cry If You Don't Laugh

Each Wednesday afternoon
is the safely accompanied time of Aunt Zhu.
"Aunt Zhu, do you feel better in these days?"
The old woman looks at me with a kind smile.
I don't want her staying on bed quite a long time
and would encourage her getting up to move.
I don't want her to survive on liquidity all day
rather let her to live more significant.
"Aunt Zhu,
you need to train your swallowing function
also the strength of your hands and feet muscles.
Has the home care physiatrist come? "
"Yes!"
"OK! So I don't worry anymore,
be relaxed and laugh frequently!
I wholeheartedly hope you happy
otherwise I will cry if you don't laugh."

淡水河邊
Beside The Tamsui River

About the Poetess

Wang Ya-ru was born in 1981 and has been working for long-term care service more than ten years. She is also specializing in dance and won a Dance Competition Award in 2019. Since 2018, she has begun to write poems and contributed her creations to the Li Poetry Magazine. Her poetry books include *"Dialogue of a Home Care Worker,* 2021*"* and *"I am in Tamsui,* 2023*"*.

About the Translator

Lee Kuei-shien (1937-2025) has published 62 poetry books in different languages, including Mandarin, Japanese, English, Portuguese, Mongol, Romanian, Russian, Spanish, French, Korean, Bengali, Serbian, Turkish, Albanian, Arabic, German and Hindi. His achievement in poetry creation has been awarded with Wu Cho-liu Award of New Poetry, Wu Yong-fu Award of Literature Criticism, Rong-hou Taiwanese Poet Prize, Lai Ho Literature Prize, Premier Culture Prize, Wu San-lien Prize in Poetry, Oxford Award for Taiwan Writers from Aletheia University, National Culture and Arts Prize of Taiwan, and many international prizes from India, Mongolia, Korea, Bangladesh, Macedonia, Peru, Montenegro, Serbia and USA.

淡水河邊

Beside The Tamsui River

語言文學類　PG3168　台灣詩叢26

淡水河邊
Beside The Tamsui River
—— 王亞茹漢英雙語詩集

作　　者 / 王亞茹（Wang Ya-ru）
譯　　者 / 李魁賢（Lee Kuei-shien）
責任編輯 / 吳霽恆
圖文排版 / 黃莉珊
封面設計 / 嚴若綾

發　行　人 / 宋政坤
法律顧問 / 毛國樑　律師
出版發行 / 秀威資訊科技股份有限公司
　　　　　114台北市內湖區瑞光路76巷65號1樓
　　　　　電話：+886-2-2796-3638　傳真：+886-2-2796-1377
　　　　　http://www.showwe.com.tw
劃撥帳號 / 19563868　戶名：秀威資訊科技股份有限公司
　　　　　讀者服務信箱：service@showwe.com.tw
展售門市 / 國家書店（松江門市）
　　　　　104台北市中山區松江路209號1樓
　　　　　電話：+886-2-2518-0207　傳真：+886-2-2518-0778
網路訂購 / 秀威網路書店：https://store.showwe.tw
　　　　　國家網路書店：https://www.govbooks.com.tw

2025年6月　BOD一版
定價：250元
版權所有　翻印必究
本書如有缺頁、破損或裝訂錯誤，請寄回更換

Copyright©2025 by Showwe Information Co., Ltd.
Printed in Taiwan
All Rights Reserved

國家圖書館出版品預行編目

淡水河邊:王亞茹漢英雙語詩集 = Beside the Tamsui River/
王亞茹著;李魁賢譯. -- 一版. -- 臺北市:秀威資訊科技
股份有限公司, 2025.06
　　面；　公分. -- (語言文學類 ; PG3168)(台灣詩叢 ; 26)
中英對照
BOD版
ISBN 978-626-7511-90-9(平裝)

863.51　　　　　　　　　　　　　　　114005458